Mary Marony
and the Snake

OTHER YEARLING BOOKS

YOU WILL ENJOY:

YEARLING BOOKS are designed especially to entertain and enlighten young people. Patricia Reilly Giff, consultant to this series, received her bachelor's degree from Marymount College and a master's degree in history from St. John's University. She holds a Professional Diploma in Reading and a Doctorate of Humane Letters from Hofstra University. She was a teacher and reading consultant for many years, and is the author of numerous books for young readers.

Suzy Kline

Mary Marony and the Snake

Illustrations by Blanche Sims

A Yearling Book

Acknowledgments
Special thanks to Dot Barlow,
speech therapist for Southwest School, and to
Michael Hickey's father, Patrick Hickey,
for bringing a garter snake
to our classroom.

Published by
Bantam Doubleday Dell Books for Young Readers
a division of
Bantam Doubleday Dell Publishing Group, Inc.
1540 Broadway
New York, New York 10036

ISBN: 0-440-41132-7

Reprinted by arrangement with G. P. Putnam's Sons, a division of The Putnam & Grosset Group

Printed in the United States of America

January 1996

10 9 8 7 6 5 4 3 2

CWO

To Francis Clarke and Doris Maier,
my speech therapists at Marin
Elementary School in Albany,
California. Thank you for helping me
in second grade like Mary Marony.
And to my BRAVE second graders
who know what it's like to have a
snake escape in the classroom.

Contents

Mary Marony and the Snake

1

Muh-mary Muh-marony

"Welcome to second grade!" Mrs. Bird said.

Mary looked at her new teacher. She *looked* like a bird. A cardinal! Her red hair was brushed back, and she had a pointed nose.

"I want each one of you to stand up, say your name, and tell us one thing about yourself," the teacher said.

Mary put her head down on the desk. She didn't want to be there. She wanted to be at her old school with her old friends and her old teacher, Mrs. Brown. They knew about her problem and understood.

Why did her parents have to buy a new house in a new neighborhood!

Mrs. Bird walked over to the first row. "Will you begin?"

"My name is Elizabeth Conway, and I like to watch TV."

Mrs. Bird didn't say anything. Everyone could tell the teacher didn't think much of TV.

A boy with big ears was next. "I'm Fred Heinz. I like catsup."

Everyone laughed.

"On hamburgers?" Mrs. Bird asked.

"Nope. I put catsup on oysters."

"Blaaaaaugh . . . ," the class groaned.

Mary counted eight people until her turn. Her stomach began to make funny noises.

"My name is Audrey Tang," a girl said.

"She likes orange juice," Fred teased.

Mrs. Bird shook her finger. "We don't make fun of each other in this class."

Mary sat up. Maybe her new teacher would understand her problem.

"What do you want to tell us, Audrey?"

"I like to make things like this," she said, holding up a necklace of beads.

Everyone looked.

"It must have taken a long time to string all those beads, Audrey," the teacher said.

Audrey nodded.

As the children stood up one by one, Mary found that it was suddenly her turn. Her lips seemed glued together.

"Next?" Mrs. Bird was looking right at Mary.

Slowly, she stood up. There was no getting out of it. She had to say her name. Now her new class would know she stuttered a little on some words.

But especially on *M* words! Why did her name have to start with two of them?

"Muh-muh-mary Muh-muh-marony."

The boy behind Mary started to giggle.

Mrs. Bird didn't notice. "What

would you like to tell us about yourself, Mary?"

"I like to r-read about animals and d-do muh-muh-math."

Why did one of her favorite things have to be an *M* word?

"I have an interesting class!" Mrs. Bird said as she moved on to the curly-haired boy behind Mary.

Mary sat down and took a deep breath. Her turn was over!

"I'm Marvin Higgins. My dad found a garter snake in our backyard."

"Really?" the teacher asked.

"Yup. Dad said he could bring it to school on Wednesday when he's fixing the telephone poles on this block. He's a telephone repairman. If it's okay with you, he could bring the snake in the morning and pick it up in the afternoon."

Mrs. Bird walked over to the terrarium that was once a fish tank. Three African violets were growing in it now. "We could put the snake in here for the day."

"Great!" Marvin said. "I'll tell Dad."

The class oohed and aahed.

Mary smiled for the first time in second grade. Maybe things wouldn't be as bad as she thought. Now she knew the boy behind her liked snakes. So did she!

Her mother found a garter snake in the garden once. She showed Mary how to pick it up by the back of its neck.

Mary turned around. "I like s-snakes too, Muh-muh-marvin," she said.

"Good for you, Muh-muh-mary," he teased.

Mary gritted her teeth. Marvin was so MEAN! He made fun of the way she said *M* words. Well, she thought, folding her arms and sinking down in her seat, it won't happen again. I'll NEVER say another *M* word to Marvin Higgins again!

A Day with No M *Words*

Mary Marony had it all planned. As long as she didn't say the *M* part of a word, she wouldn't stutter so much. And if she didn't stutter so much, brats like Marvin Higgins wouldn't tease her.

She tried her plan on her mother and father at breakfast.

"'Morning, Mary," her father said, sipping his coffee.

“ ’Orning, Dad,” she replied, sitting down at the table.

Mary waited. Her father didn’t say anything. Hurray! she thought.

“Do you want grape jelly or marmalade on your toast, dear?” Mrs. Marony asked.

"'Armalade, please."

"Coming up."

"Thanks, 'Om!" It was as easy as her mother's no-fail fudge, she thought.

When Mary got to class and the bell rang, Mrs. Bird stood in front of the blackboard. "'Morning, boys and girls."

"'Orning, is-ses Bird," Mary replied along with the class.

No one noticed.

Not even Marvin.

After the pledge, Mrs. Bird wrote the words *Creative Problem Solving* on the board. "Every day we will meet in small groups, share our ideas, and stretch our minds."

". . . like chewing gum?" Fred Heinz giggled.

"Yes, like gum," Mrs. Bird continued. She didn't seem mad. "Here's today's challenge. I want you and your group to brainstorm what you could do with an object like this."

Then she held up a piece of brown paper and folded it into the shape of a cone. "Try to come up with as many different ideas as you can."

Mary wondered who she would be with.

Mrs. Bird quickly made four groups of five and told each group to sit down in one corner of the room.

Mary sat near the terrarium with Audrey, Elizabeth, Fred, and Marvin.

Mrs. Bird gave each group a brown-paper cone. "You have fifteen minutes to share your ideas. Begin!"

Audrey studied the cone first.

"I got it," she said. "Look! I'm squeezing frosting through this cone and decorating my birthday cake."

Marvin grabbed the cone and placed it on his forehead. "I'm a unicorn!"

Elizabeth laughed. Then she put the cone next to her mouth. "GO TEAM GO!" she shouted.

Fred put the cone on his knee and stood up. "I'm the peg-leg pirate, Long John Saliva!"

"Saliva!" Everyone laughed. Even Mary.

"You mean Long John Silver," Mrs. Bird corrected. "How's everyone doing?" she asked.

"Just fine," Marvin said. "It's Mary's turn."

Mary knew why Marvin didn't tease her. The teacher was listening.

Mary took the cone. She had to think of something that didn't have an *M* word. "I g-got it!" she said. Then she put the cone next to her bottom and bent over. "Bzzzzzzz!" she sounded.

"A bee with a stinger! How clever!" Mrs. Bird exclaimed.

Marvin laughed so hard he fell over backwards.

Fred snorted and giggled.

Mary was having fun for the first time in second grade.

After Mrs. Bird left, Marvin took the cone again. He crashed it to the floor and acted like he trapped something with it. "I just caught that bee with the stinger!"

Audrey and Elizabeth leaned forward. Slowly Marvin lifted the cone. "AHA!" he said. "I squished that bee. It's dead. Too bad, Mary Marony, who eats cheese and baloney. Your bee is muh-muh-mooshed!"

So he wouldn't forget, Mary thought. "Y-you're muh-mean, Muh-muh-marvin!" Her eyes started to fill up with tears, but she was too angry to cry. Quickly she wiped them with her sleeve.

Marvin laughed.

Fred snorted.

"Time's up!" Mrs. Bird called.

Just in time, Mary thought. She wasn't keeping to her no-fail plan.

3

Marvin Goes to Jail

When the recess bell rang, the class ran outside.

Audrey and Elizabeth came over to Mary. "Do you want to play jump rope?" they asked.

"S-sure, d-do you have a jump rope?" Mary asked.

"In my purse," Audrey answered. Mary watched Audrey pull out a jump rope.

"You muh-muh-made one out of r-rubber bands?" Mary was so excited she forgot about not saying *M* words again.

"Three hundred and forty-two rubber bands," Audrey said.

"Wow!" Mary replied. "Th-that must have taken you a long t-time."

"One rainy Sunday."

"Audrey's clever like that," Elizabeth said.

As the girls turned the rope, Mary jumped in the middle. She sang the words to her favorite chant. Mary never stuttered when she sang:

MISS MARY MACK,
MACK, MACK
ALL DRESSED IN BLACK,
BLACK, BLACK
SHE ASKED HER MOTHER,
MOTHER, MOTHER
FOR FIFTY CENTS,
CENTS, CENTS
TO SEE THE ELEPHANTS,
ELEPHANTS,
ELEPHANTS . . .

Suddenly Marvin jumped out from behind the dumpster. "CHARGE!" he yelled and ran right through the girls' game, taking the jump rope with him.

"Muh-muh-marvin makes me s-so muh-muh-muh-mad!" Mary said. Then she covered her mouth.

Audrey looked at Mary and smiled. "Let's go get it back!"

"Yes!" said Elizabeth.

"Yes!" said Mary.

The girls ran across the playground looking for Marvin. There he was! Leaning against the brick wall, dangling the rubber-band jump rope in front of him.

"CHARGE!" Mary yelled.

"CHARGE!" Elizabeth and Audrey repeated. The three girls ran toward Marvin. As soon as he saw the girl-attack, he stuffed the jump rope in his pocket and took off across the diamond.

"HEY! GET OUT OF OUR KICKBALL GAME!" Fred hollered.

Marvin jumped over the rolling red ball and ran past the outfielders.

The girls chased after him.

When Marvin got to the tetherball court, he ducked just in time.

WHISH! The flying white ball whirled around.

The girls just missed it too.

When Marvin ran around the corner, he came to a brick wall. There was no place to go. Marvin was trapped!

Elizabeth grabbed one arm.

Audrey grabbed the other.

"LET ME GO!" Marvin shouted.

"Not until you give up the rope," Mary said.

"NO WAY, JOSE!" Marvin shouted.

"Then we'll take y-you to JAIL!" Mary said.

"Jail? Ha! Ha! Ha!" Marvin scoffed. "I'm not giving you any rope, Muh-mary Muh-marony!"

Audrey put her nose next to Marvin's. "You shouldn't make fun of people who stutter. That's being mean."

"Yeah," Elizabeth agreed. "That goes DOUBLE for me too."

Mary smiled at her two new friends. They understood her problem. She didn't have to have any plan. She could be herself.

"Hand over the r-rope, Muh-marvin!" Mary demanded.

"NO WAY, JOSE!" Marvin repeated.

"Okay, Marvin, you are going to jail!" Audrey said. Then she whispered to Mary. "Where's the jail?"

Mary pointed to the garbage can.

The girls laughed.

"HERE WE GO!" they shouted. And they picked up Marvin's feet and arms and carried him to the garbage can.

"One. . . two. . . three!" they counted.

KERPLOP!

The girls stuffed Marvin into the garbage can.

"Eeeweee! Get me out of here! There's banana peels and smelly egg sandwiches in here!"

Mary held out her hand. "The r-rope, please."

Marvin reached into his pocket and pulled out a fistful of rubber bands. "HERE!"

Audrey took it. "It is still in one piece."

"Good," Mary replied.

"YOU HAVE TO HELP ME OUT OF HERE . . . NOW!" Marvin screamed.

The girls put their arms around each other and made a huddle. After they whispered something, they faced Marvin. "NO WAY, JOSE!" they called.

Then they ran back across the playground holding hands.

4

Going Undercover

The next morning Mary was brushing her hair and counting each brush stroke. "Ninety-six, ninety-seven, ninety-eight, ninety-nine . . ."

"Your hair glistens!" her mother said. Then she handed Mary two barrettes in the shape of bluebirds. "I found them on the bathroom floor."

"Th-thanks, Muh-mom," Mary said snapping them into place.

"You're welcome. Can we talk?"

Mary put her brush down. "Wh-what is it?"

"Your teacher called last night when you were in bed."

"About muh-me?"

"Yes."

"What d-did she say?" Mary wondered if it was going to be about Marvin in the garbage can.

"She said she read your file folder and

a note that was put there by your last year's teacher."

"W-what did Mrs. Brown say about muh-me?"

"Mrs. Brown said you should see a speech therapist."

"What's th-that?"

"A speech therapist helps children who sometimes have trouble talking."

Mary raised her voice. "NO! NEVER! N-NEVER! N-NOT IN A MUH-MUH-MILLION YEARS!"

Then she jumped into her bed, fully dressed, and pulled the bedspread over herself.

Mrs. Marony walked around to the other side of the bed, crawled in, and pulled the bedspread over herself. Clothes, high heels, and all!

"We can talk undercover if you like," Mrs. Marony said.

Mary liked that. It was safe under the bedspread. And dark and cozy. She loved the smell of her mother's lilac perfume.

"Can we whisper?" Mary asked. She knew she didn't stutter when she whispered.

"Yes."

"Mrs. Brown thinks I talk terrible?"

"No, dear. She just wants you to get a little help with your stuttering."

Mary started to cry. She put her head on her mother's shoulder.

Mrs. Marony put her arm around Mary. "Did I tell you that I went to a speech therapist when I was in second grade?"

Mary stopped crying and sat up. She tucked the bedspread behind her to make a tent.

"You stuttered, Muh-mom?"

"It runs in our family. My dad did too."

"Did you stutter more on *M* words like me?"

Mrs. Marony sat up. "No, but I had trouble with *K* words, and *D* words, and *I* words, and *W* words. I really hated *W* words."

"I hate *M* words," Mary whispered. Then she had to wipe her nose on the bedspread. “How come you don’t stutter now?”

“Because my second-grade teacher sent me to a speech therapist, and she really helped me. In two years, I was speaking like everyone else. I just stuttered when I was nervous or afraid.”

“You mean someday I’ll be able to say *M* words?”

“Mary, you can say some *M* words now. The speech therapist will help you say ALL your words better.”

Mary hugged her mother and then rolled out of bed. “I’d better go to school!”

Mrs. Marony threw back the bedspread. “I’d better go to work!”

When they both saw themselves in the mirror, they laughed.

“What a muh-muh-mess we are!” Mary said.

5

The Arrival of the Snake and the Speech Therapist

When Mary got to the classroom that morning, Mrs. Bird was talking to Marvin's father.

He was carrying a coffee can. "Our little friend is in here. We put holes in the lid so he could breathe. Marv and I caught a few crickets for his breakfast. He won't be hungry."

Everyone gathered around the science table and watched.

"Was it hard to catch him in your garden?" Audrey asked Marvin.

Marvin shivered. "I don't pick up snakes. Dad caught it for me."

The class watched Mr. Higgins lower the garter snake into the terrarium. The striped tail wiggled and wriggled back and forth. As soon as the snake touched the dirt, it slithered away. Mr. Higgins closed the lid. Quickly, Mrs. Bird taped some foil over the small opening in the back.

"Do you think this tank will be safe enough?" Mrs. Bird asked Mr. Higgins.

"That should do it," he said. Then he bent down and tapped the glass. "Have fun in second grade. Pay attention, Herman!"

The class laughed. They liked the snake's name.

Mr. Higgins waved good-bye. "I'll be back around two o'clock when I'm finished fixing the telephone poles on this block."

"Bye, Dad!" Marvin called out.

As the children watched Herman slither in and out of the African violets, a tall visitor came to the door.

It was a woman wearing stoplight earrings. Mary thought the red, yellow, and green stones were fun to look at.

"Miss Lawton! Come on in!" Mrs. Bird said. "We were just observing our garter snake."

Miss Lawton came over to the terrarium and looked in. "How long will he be in your classroom?"

"Just for the day," Mrs. Bird answered.

"That's the speech therapist," Audrey whispered in Mary's ear. "She's nice."

Mary tried to smile at the beautiful lady when Mrs. Bird introduced her. But it was hard. Especially when she invited Mary to her office. Mary just wanted to stay in her own classroom with her own friends and watch the snake.

Reluctantly, she followed the lady down the hall and into a small room. When she got inside she looked around. It wasn't like an office. There were puppets and puzzles on one table. A pink telephone and stuffed animals on another. There was a big shelf of games and lots of pictures on the wall.

"Sit down, Mary," Miss Lawton said in a slow, clear voice.

Mary did. She felt comfortable.

"You and I will get to visit and talk twice a week for twenty-five minutes. I think it will be fun. Do you like zoos?" she asked, pointing to the picture of the chimpanzee.

Mary finally smiled. "Yes. I l-like to r-read about animals. I love muh-muh-monkeys and . . ."

Mary stopped talking. She was embarrassed. She had stuttered on an *M* word.

"I like monkeys too," Miss Lawton replied slowly. "Does it make you feel bad to stutter, Mary?"

Mary wanted to cry. She nodded her head.

"Does anyone make fun of you when you stutter?"

"S-sometimes."

"I understand how you feel."

Miss Lawton held up a letter card. "What sound does this *M* make?"

"Muh?" Mary said.

"M-mmmmmmmmm," Miss Lawton corrected. "Watch my lips. Mmmmmmmmmmm."

Mary repeated the sound, "Mmmmmmmmmmm."

"Say 'Mmmmmmmary.'"

"Mmmmmmmmary."

"Good! Now say, 'Mmmmary is here.'"

"Mmmmary is here."

"Mary is here on Mmmmmondays."

Mary took a deep breath. She tried to talk slowly and clearly like Miss Lawton did. "Mmmmary is here on Mmmmondays."

"Wonderful!"

Mary beamed. "I like saying 'mmmmmmm.' Do you know th-that mmmmmmmm-good s-soup commercial on TV?"

Miss Lawton laughed.

After Mary talked, hummed, laughed, and played with the animal puppets for twenty-five minutes, she returned to class.

6

The Snake Escapes!

At 2:30 that afternoon, Mr. Higgins showed up at the classroom door. He had lots of copper wire and phone cords hanging from his pants pockets, and he had a bag of tools on his back. "How's our friend?" he asked.

Mrs. Bird looked happy to see him. "It's funny. Herman's dug such a hole for himself, we haven't seen him since lunchtime."

“Really?” Mr. Higgins laughed. “Snakes can be sneaky.” Then he took off the lid and fished around the terrarium for the snake.

Everyone gathered around the science table and watched. Mrs. Bird did too.

A minute later, Marvin said, “Did he get out, Dad?”

"That can't be!" Mrs. Bird cried. "I put tape around the one small opening in the back."

"There's a tear here," Mr. Higgins said, pointing to the foil.

Mrs. Bird leaned over to see. "Oh my goodness!"

Mr. Higgins picked up the terrarium. "I'll tell you what. Let me take this thing outside to the front lawn. I'll dump everything out. If Herman's in here, I'll find him."

Mrs. Bird closed her eyes. It looked like she was saying a quick prayer. "Okay, boys and girls, return to your seats now."

She walked over to the wall map and pulled it down. "Who can tell me where Washington, D.C., is?"

Marvin went up and tried, but he

pointed to the state of Washington.

"Is that correct, class?" Mrs. Bird asked.

Mary went up and showed Marvin where Washington, D.C., was.

At that moment Mr. Higgins carried the terrarium back into the classroom. His hands were covered with dirt. "I took everything out. That snake is *not* in here! I'm sorry, Mrs. Bird. The snake escaped!"

"THE SNAKE ESCAPED!" Elizabeth yelled.

The class shrieked.

"Now, boys and girls," Mrs. Bird said, "let's st-stay c-calm. Just d-don't leave your seats. Mr. Higgins and I will l-look around."

Mary knew her teacher was nervous. Now *she* was stuttering.

Mr. Higgins got on his knees and crawled around the room.

Mrs. Bird followed him. When she saw something curled up in the corner, she jumped. "OH!" she exclaimed.

Mr. Higgins reached for it. Then he held up some curly phone cord. "Must have fallen out of my pocket."

Mrs. Bird took a deep breath.

"Over there!" Audrey called out. "By the wastepaper basket."

Everyone turned.

Mr. Higgins hurried over. He grabbed the striped thing and held it up.

"A hair ribbon!" the class replied.

It belonged to Elizabeth.

Mrs. Bird ran her fingers through her red hair. "That snake has to be h-here somewhere!"

Mary was still standing in front of the class with Marvin. They were both next to the map. Suddenly she saw something moving along the chalk tray.

She looked again.

It was the snake!

Why were there so many *M* words to say, she thought! But this was an emergency. She had to say them. Slowly and clearly like Miss Lawton had shown her.

"Mmmmmmm," she hummed. "Mmmm move, mmmmmm Marvin! The s-snake is behind the mmmmmmm map!"

Marvin jumped two feet in the air!

His curly hair was standing on end!

Mary grabbed the snake behind its head like her mother had taught her. Then she held it up for Mr. Higgins to see. "Here," she said as the snake wiggled and wriggled its tail back and forth.

The class shivered in their seats.

Mrs. Bird dashed over to Mary.

Mr. Higgins took the snake and popped it into the coffee can.

Marvin sat down in his chair. His teeth were chattering, and his curls were shaking.

Mrs. Bird put her arm around Mary. "I think we have a very brave student in our class," she said.

"She sure is!" Mr. Higgins replied as he put the plastic lid on the coffee can.

"I think we should give Mary a big hand for finding our snake and saving us all from lots of worry," Mrs. Bird said. "Take a bow, Mary Marony."

Everyone clapped.

Even Marvin.

Mary smiled. Things were starting to be okay in second grade. "Thank you very muh-muh-much," she said.